E.S.E.A. TITLE IV

Bright Fawn and Me

by *Jay Leech and Zane Spencer*

illustrated by Glo Coalson

Thomas Y. Crowell • New York

To our own siblings, who like everything we write

— Jay Leech and Zane Spencer

Bright Fawn and Me
Text copyright © 1979 by Jay Leech and Zane Spencer
Illustrations copyright © 1979 by Glo Coalson
All rights reserved. Printed in the United States of America.
No part of this book may be used or reproduced in any manner
whatsoever without written permission except in the case of
brief quotations embodied in critical articles and reviews.
For information address Thomas Y. Crowell, 10 East 53 Street,
New York, N.Y. 10022. Published simultaneously in Canada by
Fitzhenry & Whiteside Limited, Toronto.

LIBRARY OF CONGRESS CATALOGING IN PUBLICATION DATA
Leech, Jay. Bright Fawn and me.
SUMMARY: An Indian girl considers her younger
sister a pest, but doesn't like other children to call her one.
[1. Brothers and sisters—Fiction. 2. Indians of
North America—Fiction] I. Spencer, Zane,
joint author. II. Coalson, Glo. III. Title.
PZ7.L515Br   [E]   78-19215
ISBN 0-690-03937-9   ISBN 0-690-03938-7 lib. bdg.

FIRST EDITION

This is a story of two little Cheyenne sisters who lived many days' journey south of the old trading camp on Horse Creek near the North Platte River in western Nebraska. It is not a true story. But, something like it might have happened, and probably did, more than one hundred years ago.

The trading fair was real. There, for one moon, Indians from many tribes came together in peace. They traded, danced, played games and held contests. Around the camp fires at night they told and retold stories, made new friends and renewed old acquaintances. It was a time of great joy.

I have a sister. Her name is Bright Fawn.
She shares my sleeping robe with me.
She never folds it up. Instead she plays with her doll.
I tell my mother.
My mother says, "She is little. She will learn."

My mother says to my sister and me,
"Hurry now. We must load the
travois. We want to get to the
trading fair before dark."
So I fold the buffalo sleeping robe
all by myself.
My sister does not help.
She plays with her doll.

The pack dogs are waiting, so my
mother harnesses them.
This is the last day of our long
journey.

Bright Fawn is little.
She rides on the travois and
plays with her doll.
I am big, so I must walk.

All day I walk with the people of my tribe.
We are happy, for at the trading fair all tribes
come together in peace.

The sun is red and low in the sky when we get to the
trading camp. My mother says, "We must hurry and
set up our lodge before darkness comes."

With the morning sun my mother says,
"Take Bright Fawn for a walk.
I must prepare food for the great feast."
So I take my sister for a walk.
She wants to hold my hand.
I let her.

We pass the lodge of my grandmother.
She is also preparing food for the great feast.
She smiles at Bright Fawn and me and says,
"I have a treat for you."
She gives me two elk-horn spoons with
honey in them. "Hoye!" I cry. "Thank you."

I give one to Bright Fawn and keep one for me.
A dog takes Bright Fawn's. She starts to cry.
I tell the dog to get away.
He goes, but Bright Fawn does not stop crying.
I give her my honey.

We see my friend Lost Star. She is watching the
young braves run footraces.
She raises her hand in greeting, and I raise mine.
She asks me why my hand is all sticky and brown.
I tell her Bright Fawn always hangs on to me.
Lost Star says, "I wish I had a sister."
"I wish I had some honey," I tell her,
and give Bright Fawn a mean look.
Bright Fawn smiles at me.
Lost Star says, "She is a nice little sister."

We walk down the main path of the trading fair.
Bright Fawn cannot keep up with me.
We stop beside a man from a western tribe.
He has many fur robes to trade.
He says, "You have a fine little sister."
"She is slow," I say. "She cannot walk as
fast as I can."
The man from the west says, "She is little.
She will learn."

We pass the maidens going to the river for water.
They giggle and pretend they do not see the young
braves beside the path.
One maiden stops and says to me, "You have a fine
little sister."
I pretend I do not hear.

We see a brave on a horse.
Bright Fawn starts to cry.
I say, "What is wrong now?"
She says she wants to ride the brave's horse.
I tell her, "Nobody can ride a brave's horse
except a brave."
I say it loud so everybody can hear.

The brave comes over and asks me what is wrong.
I tell him my dumb sister wants to ride his horse.
The brave smiles at Bright Fawn. He says,
"A little girl with honey on her chin should not cry."
He lets Bright Fawn sit on his horse.
He tells me I am lucky to have such a fine
little sister.

I try to wipe the honey off Bright Fawn's chin.
She will not let me.
I tell her to wipe her own chin then.
She does not.
She just hangs on tight to my hand and smiles at me.

We walk by the lodge of a tall man from the north.
He has many strong bows for trading.
He pats Bright Fawn on the head.
Bright Fawn smiles and the man says to me,
"You have a fine little sister."

We walk by the trees.
My sister stubs her toe on a root.
"Pick up your feet," I say.
"You might fall down and break your head."
I say it loud so everybody will hear.

We pass a papoose who sleeps in his cradleboard.
His mother is beside him.
She has many bright stones for trading.
She has colored capes made of feathers.
"You are lucky to have such a happy little sister,"
she says.
I do not say anything.

"Come to the dancing with me,"
a girl calls.
I tell her I have to watch my
sister instead.
Bright Fawn laughs up at me and
licks at the honey on her chin.
"Let her dance, too," the girl says.
I tell her Bright Fawn is too
little to dance.
"She is too little to do anything,"
I say. "She is a pest."

"We could play hide and seek on
the way. Maybe the pest will hide,
and we will not be able to find her."
The girl winks at me and
ducks behind a bush.

I look at my sister with the honey on her chin.
I look back at the girl as she peeks around the bush.
"You are not nice," I say.
"You call Bright Fawn a pest."

The girl laughs and pulls a handful of leaves off the bush. She tosses them at Bright Fawn and me. "You call her a pest, too," she says.

I brush the leaves off Bright Fawn's dress.
"See, she cannot even brush the leaves off herself,"
the girl says.
I look down at Bright Fawn.
I look back at the girl.
Then I say, "She is little. She will learn."
"Just the same," the girl says. "I am glad I do not
have a sister."

I look down at Bright Fawn.
I look over at the girl.
I stick out my tongue at the girl.

I take Bright Fawn's hand.
I squeeze it tight in mine.
And we walk down the path of the great
trading fair together.

E
Lee   c l
      Leech, Fay   20275

   BRIGHT FAWN AND ME

FEB 7	DATE DUE		
FEB 16	DEC 21	4	
FEB 23	OCT 17		
NOV 8	MAR 17		
JAN 10	SEP 2 3		
NOV 2 0	MAR 1		
JAN 2 1	MAR 17		
137	OCT 1		
134	135		
APR 8			
127			
130			